Dear Parent:

Do you want to spark your child's creativity? Do you want your child to become a confident writer? Road to Writing can help.

Road to Writing is a unique creative writing program that gives even the youngest writers a chance to express themselves. Featuring five distinct levels, or Miles, the Road to Writing program accompanies children from their first attempts at writing to comfortably writing on their own.

 A Creative Start
For children who "write" stories by drawing pictures
• easy picture prompts • familiar subjects • places to draw

 Creative Writing With Help
For children who write easy words with help
• detailed picture prompts • places to draw and label

 Creative Writing On Your Own
For children who write simple sentences on their own
• basic story starters • popular topics • places to write

 First Journals
For children who are comfortable writing short paragraphs
• more complex story starters • space for free writing

 Journals
For children who want to try different kinds of writing
• cues for poems, jokes, stories • brainstorming pages

There's no need to hurry through the Miles. Road to Writing is designed without age or grade levels. Children can progress at their own speed, developing confidence and pride in their writing ability along the way.

Road to Writing—"write"

Tips for Using this Book

- Read each page aloud to your child. Then let your child draw a response—right in the book!

- Don't worry—there are no "right" or "wrong" answers. This book is a place for your child to be creative.

- If your child wants to skip ahead, that's fine. It's okay to jump from page to page.

- Remember to encourage your child with lots of praise.

Pencils, pens, and crayons are all suitable for use in this book. Markers are not recommended.

A GOLDEN BOOK • New York
Golden Books Publishing Company, Inc. New York, New York 10106

ISBN: 0-307-45608-0

10 9 8 7 6 5 4 3 2

Seasons

by Carol Pugliano-Martin and

_____

(your name)

illustrated by
Geneviève Leloup and

_____

(your name)

WINTER

Draw your favorite winter hat.

Draw a wacky
new winter coat.

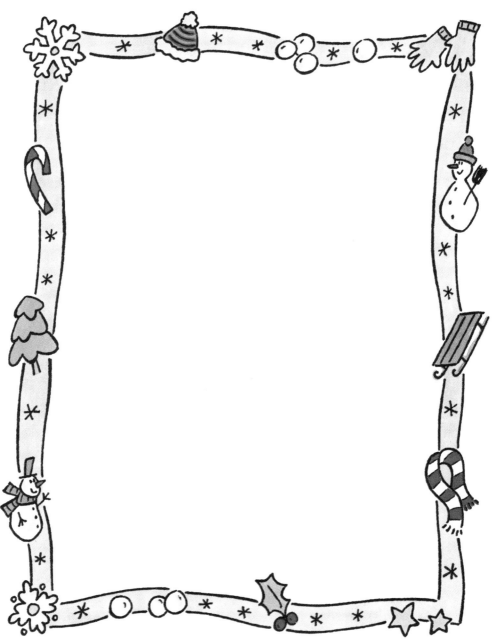

Make up your own ending
to the story.

Draw it.

The Snow Man

by _____

1.

2.

3.

Every snowflake looks
different.

Draw your own snowflake.

Oh, no! There was a snowstorm.
How will you get to school?

Pick one, or make up your own.

by ice skates

by sled

by snowboard

by _____

Draw yourself getting to school one of these ways.

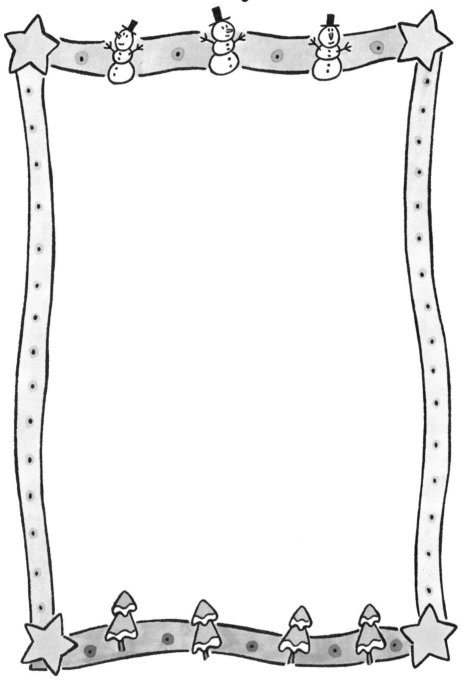

Draw an animal
that likes the snow.

Draw an animal that does *not* like the snow.

Hot cocoa tastes great
on a cold winter day.

Draw your own cocoa mug.

What else do you do
to keep warm in the winter?

Draw yourself doing it.

It's Groundhog Day.
The groundhog saw its shadow.
So did you!

Draw your shadow.

Draw your best friend's shadow.

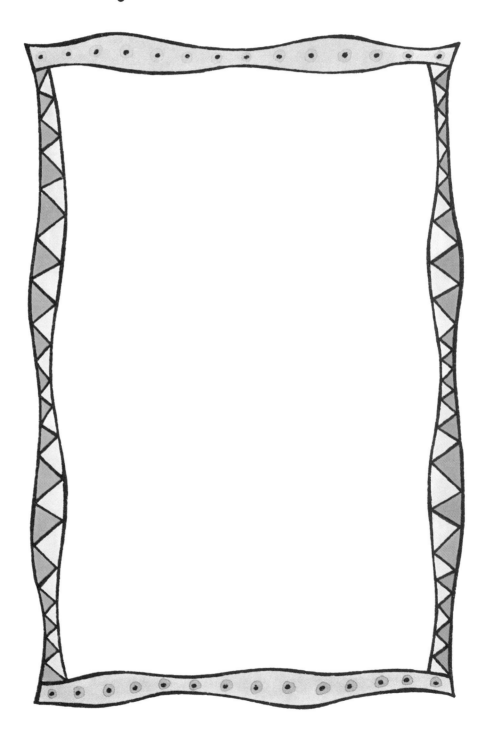

SPRING

Draw a garden that grows all your favorite foods.

Something scary is growing
in your garden.

Draw it.

April showers!
Draw your favorite
thing to do on a
rainy day.

If you decide to go outdoors,
draw what you will need
to stay dry.

This caterpillar is in its cocoon.

Draw what it will look like as a butterfly.

Make up your own ending
to the story.

Draw it.

by _____

1.

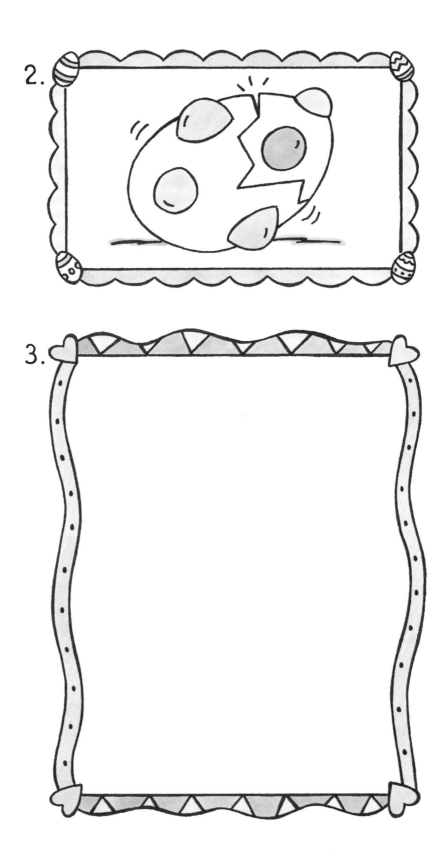

Go fly a kite!
Design your own kite.

Draw yourself flying it.

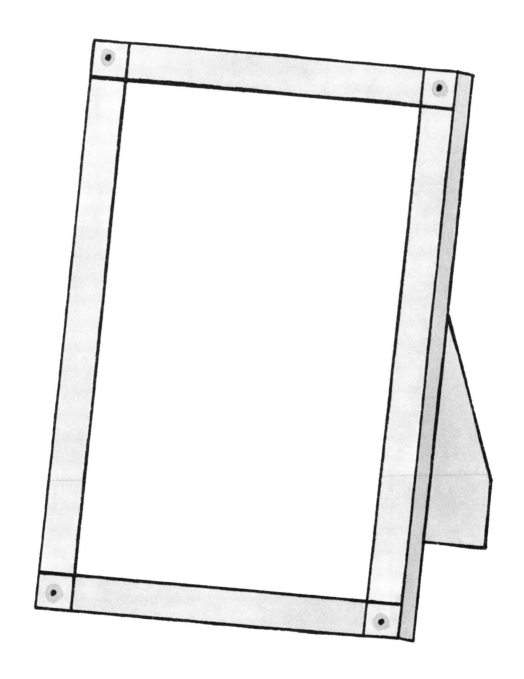

SUMMER

You are going to the beach. What will you pack in your beach bag?

Draw yourself at the beach.

What do you like
to do in the summer?

Draw yourself doing it.

What *don't* you like
to do in the summer?

Draw yourself doing it.

Ice cream tastes great on a hot summer day.

Make your own sundae.

What else do you do to keep cool in the summer?

Draw yourself doing it.

Make up your own ending
to the story.

Draw it.

by _____

1.

2.

3.

You won the sandcastle contest.

Draw the sandcastle you built.

Draw the prize you won.

FALL

You are going pumpkin picking.

Draw a field full of pumpkins.

Pick a pumpkin.

Decorate it for Halloween.

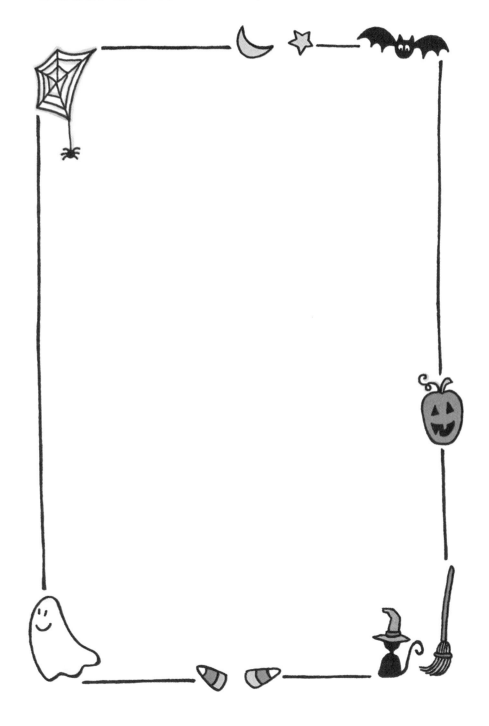

Happy Halloween!
Draw yourself and your
friends in your
Halloween costumes.

You got lots of trick-or-treat goodies.

Draw them in your Halloween bag.

It's apple picking time.
What yummy foods can you
make from apples?

_____   _____

_____   _____

Draw the different foods.

It's Thanksgiving!
Draw the food
on the table.

What's your favorite season?

_____

Draw something that makes you think of that season.